Ducks

Kate Riggs

CREATIVE EDUCATION
CREATIVE PAPERBACKS

seedlings

Published by Creative Education and Creative Paperbacks
P.O. Box 227, Mankato, Minnesota 56002
Creative Education and Creative Paperbacks are imprints of
The Creative Company
www.thecreativecompany.us

Design by Ellen Huber; production by Dana Cheit
Art direction by Rita Marshall
Printed in the United States of America

Photographs by Alamy (Matthew Fry), Dreamstime (Larussylvestris), iStockphoto (Andyworks, Artex67, bazilfoto, GlobalP, Jevtic, MikeLane45, Tamilisa Miner, mirceax, NatalyaAksenova, puflic_senior, randimal, SvetaVo, taviphoto, TT, Valengilda, valentinrussanov), Shutterstock (Sandi Cullifer, Alexander Erdbeer, shanov, E. Spek)

Library of Congress Cataloging-in-Publication Data
Names: Riggs, Kate, author.
Title: Ducks / Kate Riggs.
Series: Seedlings: Backyard Animals.
Includes bibliographical references and index.
Summary: A kindergarten-level introduction to ducks, covering their growth process, behaviors, the watery habitats they call home, and such defining features as their webbed feet.
Identifiers: LCCN 2017051384 / ISBN 978-1-60818-970-0 (hardcover) / ISBN 978-1- 62832-597-3 (pbk) / ISBN 978-1-64000-071-1 (eBook)

Subjects: LCSH: Ducks—Juvenile literature.
Classification: LCC SF505.3.R54 2018 / DDC 636.5/97—dc23

CCSS: RI.K.1, 2, 3, 4, 5, 6, 7; RI.1.1, 2, 3, 4, 5, 6, 7; RF.K.1, 3; RF.1.1

First Edition HC 9 8 7 6 5 4 3 2 1
First Edition PBK 9 8 7 6 5 4 3 2 1

TABLE OF CONTENTS

Hello, ducks!

Feathered ducks are waterbirds. They swim in small ponds and big lakes.

Some ducks swim by the sea.

A duck has a **bill**.

It has two **webbed** feet for swimming.

Strong wings help it fly.

Ducks can be many colors.

Males are more colorful than females.

Male mallards have shiny green heads.

Ducks eat water plants, fish, and bugs.

They find seeds, berries, and worms on land.

Young ducklings have soft, fluffy feathers. These are called down.

Ducklings follow their mother.

Ducks dabble or dive.

They call to each other.

They waddle away.

Goodbye, ducks!

Picture a Duck

feathers

bill
female mallard
upper wing coverts
speculum

Words to Know

bill: the flattened beak of a duck or other web-footed bird

dabble: to feed by moving the bill around in shallow water

webbed: having toes connected by flat skin

Read More

Kawa, Katie. *Ducklings.*
New York: Gareth Stevens, 2012.

Leaf, Christina. *Baby Ducks.*
Minneapolis: Bellwether Media, 2015.

Websites

First School: Duck Theme Preschool Activities and Crafts
http://www.first-school.ws/theme/animals/birds/duck.htm
Print out coloring pages and crafts to have more fun with ducks.

National Geographic Kids: Mallard Duck
https://kids.nationalgeographic.com/animals/mallard-duck
/#mallard-male-swimming.jpg
Learn more about this common kind of duck.

Note: Every effort has been made to ensure that the websites listed above are suitable for children, that they have educational value, and that they contain no inappropriate material. However, because of the nature of the Internet, it is impossible to guarantee that these sites will remain active indefinitely or that their contents will not be altered.

Index